Disclaimer: These stories are works of fiction; any resemblance to real people, names, or events is coincidental and unintentional. All characters are well over the age of 18. Absolutely no minors may read these works. Please note, these stories contain elements of BDSM and sex, including vaginal, anal, and oral sex, whipping, electro-stimulation, shaving, ticking, indentured servitude (voluntary slavery,) and other adult-oriented material. Do not read this collection of erotica if doing so is illegal in your jurisdiction or you find these subjects to be against your moral standards. With that being said, please enjoy.

Story One: *The Gift*

Master was late. Skye glanced at the clock on the wall repeatedly. Five minutes past six, then fifteen. She paced around the foyer a few times, then double-checked everything else was perfect. It *had* to be perfect; Master would accept no disorder around the house. It wasn't until nearly a quarter to seven when she finally heard the familiar sound of the V-8 from his Corvette as he slowly rolled up the driveway. She hurriedly assumed the position; the same one she displayed every evening when Edgar arrived.

The twenty-eight-year-old legal assistant had the luxury of arriving home before her husband, especially since her office was only five minutes from their spacious home. She would use that time to straighten up the place, shower, perfume, and prepare her body to please her husband, lover, and master. Seven years her senior, the ophthalmologist kept regular hours, albeit later than hers, which was advantageous to them both.

Wearing only a red bra and matching, frilly-lace panties, Skye knelt on the small throw rug in the hallway leading to the front door. They had been together for five years and their dominant-submissive relationship was nothing new to them, but Skye still felt a shiver of excitement every time her husband walked through the door. Her heart thumped as much as the first time she laid her eyes on him. Every day was like being in love for the first time. Breathlessly, she watched the knob turn and saw his shiny, black shoes enter first, for her eyes were downcast and her head bowed in reverence.

"Good evening, Master," Skye said dutifully. The brunette with curly hair and crystal-blue eyes felt a slight pulse of excitement travel to her pussy just from uttering the words. Her hands clasped each other behind her flawless back.

"Hello, Baby Doll," he said as he put away his overcoat in the closet. "I'm sorry I'm so late. I-273 is a complete mess with construction and they shut down the bypass due to an accident."

"I'm just happy you're home safe, my love," Skye said, stealing a glance at his square jaw. The handsome doctor had dark, slicked-back hair and the hint of a five o'clock shadow. His dark, piercing eyes intimidated most, but she knew he had a tender side to him, even when he would tan her ass with a riding crop. "Dinner's ready; I kept it warm in the oven."

"You're so good to me," he said, leaning over to kiss the top of her head. He inhaled deeply, enjoying the scent of her freshly washed hair. He would be drinking in a different scent soon enough, but dinner awaited them. She waited respectfully until he passed her before she followed close behind.

A lot of this ritual, this routine, was Skye's idea. Her husband was naturally dominant, but his experience in BDSM never ventured much beyond tying his former girlfriends' wrists to bed posts and having his way with them. Skye, a much more adventurous and vivacious submissive, found herself often lost in spicy erotica where the archetypal 1950's husband and wife relationship existed, but with a much kinkier bend. Living her dream of marrying a rich and well-respected, dashingly handsome and exquisitely masculine man only helped fuel her desires to live out her fantasies with her loving husband.

She started it. Skye nudged him into this lifestyle. It wasn't until the second year of their marriage when she proposed the idea of being a sexual servant to his every whim. He was reluctant to the idea of treating his wife in such an archaic way living in 2020. He wondered what his friends and family would think of him if they knew his wife gave him foot rubs every evening after dinner, or how he owned a veritable arsenal of sex toys to tease and torment his beloved wife. Those fears began to subside, though, because his stunning and demure betrothed played into the role so perfectly, so willingly, he often wondered who was controlling whom.

She opened the oven and produced to plates of baked ham, mashed potatoes with gravy, and a green bean and bacon casserole. "Which wine would you like with your dinner tonight, Master?"

"The white zinfandel should pair nicely with ham," he said.

"Of course, Master," she said with a curtsey. She opened their wine fridge and selected the right bottle, returning with glasses and the corkscrew. Four years ago, he would have been uncomfortable seeing his own wife waiting on him hand and foot, pouring his wine and wearing naught but her most scandalous undies, but now, they couldn't have even fathomed a different kind of lifestyle.

"That's good," he said as she poured. She then poured an equal serving for herself and they began to enjoy their dinner.

"I'm sorry it's a bit dry from warming in the oven," she apologized.

"It's my fault for being late," he said dismissively.

"No, Master, there's nothing you could have done about the traffic. I'd rather you be late than get into an accident trying to hurry home."

He smiled at that. "I did get us a present, though, for tonight. Something I think you'll really, *really* enjoy, Baby Doll."

"I would enjoy anything from you, Master. I can't wait!"

"Neither can I," he chuckled. He stared into her light blue eyes with confidence and command. Though most men would have had a hard time forming words with a brunette bombshell who was practically naked, he only stared into her soulful eyes. It was almost as if his gaze was hypnotic; daring her to look away.

The conversation then turned into one any married couple across the country might have. They talked about work, the minor inconveniences they dealt with throughout the day, and even discussed what color siding they should redo their house with, all the while, his intense gaze never seemed to falter. Skye was already all but naked, but she always felt even more undressed whenever her husband stared at her so commandingly. She was convinced he could read her mind or see into her soul, and the thing which frightened her the most...was that she absolutely loved it.

Edgar, for his part, was madly in love with his gorgeous wife. There was something so perfectly submissive, yet sultry about her composure. She had the kind of demure confidence of a 1940s actress; Katherine Hepburn, Ingrid Bergman. The kind of classy strength that melted when the right man came along, and he was so thankful to be that man. They finished their meal and she cleared away the dishes and cleaned up the kitchen.

"Shall I give you your nightly foot rub, Master?" she asked, eager to please. She enjoyed rubbing his feet and watching his look of pure satisfaction as she knelt on the floor, giving her husband her undivided attention.

"Not today, Baby Doll. I'm kind of excited to show you the new toy I purchased."

"As you wish, Master," she said. There was the slightest twinge of disappointment in her voice. He knew she enjoyed pleasuring his feet with her deft fingers, but he wondered if she even had some sort of foot fetish based on her reaction. Nevertheless, he was too excited to dwell on the thought; another time, he might test her on the subject.

"I want you to walk up the stairs ahead of me this time. I like staring at that gorgeous ass of yours. Wiggle it seductively like I know you can."

"Yes, sir!" she replied eagerly. He watched as her butt wiggled with her tight, red panties concealing very little of her voluptuous body. She was curvy in all the right places, and perhaps even had a bit excess weight, but it was more real estate for his hand to spank or his whip to mark up. Theirs was a relationship of endless love for each other, though an outsider might see things differently based on their dynamics. Edgar's cock stIrred as he watched her sexy swagger as they went up the stairs.

Skye entered the bedroom and immediately knelt in front of the bed with her hands behind her back. "Stand up for me," he demanded and she immediately sprang to her feet. "Undo your bra," he then commanded her, and she unhooked the clasp, freeing her 44-DD sized breasts. Her smooth, dark, red areolas were punctuated by pert nipples which were already erect. No matter how many times he saw his wife's breasts, he couldn't help but ogle them.

"Jiggle them around for me, show me your goods," Edar said.

"Yes, Master," she complied. Her hands pressed her two, melon-sized tits together and she rubbed the fleshy orbs against one another. Using her hands, she lifted the undersides of her breasts up and let them back down, jiggling them back and forth.

"Mm," her master groaned with pleasure. "Now, roll those nipples for me between your fingers. Just like that. Good girl," he said. Her tongue stuck out and she saucily licked her ruby-red lips with pleasure. "Now, give them a bit of a pinch, babe."

"Ooh," she exclaimed.

"Tug on them. Pull a little farther, a little farther, squeeze harder...now hold...good girl, let them go," he ordered. Her nipples were elongated for a few seconds and turned reddish from her self-abuse.

"Oh," she groaned as the blood rushed back in to her sensitive nubs.

"How did that feel?"

"So good, Master, thank you."

"Good girl," he said. "Now, remove those panties for me and give them to me."

"Yes, Master," she said, and slid out of the red panties. He could see a wet spot on the fabric, and when she handed them to him, he put them to his nose and inhaled deeply.

"Someone is really enjoying herself tonight," he said wickedly.

"Yes, Master, quite so."

"Good, then you'll really enjoy what I have in store for you tonight, angel."

His words were like jolts of electricity coursing through her veins. His deep, commanding voice was so confident and controlling, yet also loving and tender. He was the perfect man for her. Zeus could have descended from Mount Olympus in all his Greek god glory, and her eyes would still be locked on her husband.

"On the bed, assume a spread-eagle position, face up," he ordered sternly.

"Yes, Master!" she immediately replied. Skye laid on her back and spread her arms and legs outward. Master Edgar climbed on the bed and affixed shackles to her ankles and cuffs to her wrists, leaving her vulnerable and completely at the whim of her husband's desire. She had taken this position countless times and her husband always found ways to tease, torment, and tantalize the brunette beauty, but this time felt *different* for some reason. There was a sort of energy and excitement exuding from her husband which was unusual for the normally stoic and calm man. He seemed almost giddy to try out the present he purchased for her, and it made his wife both nervous and eagerly anxious at once.

"Now, don't go anywhere, I'll be right back while I fetch your present," he said wagging his finger.

"I wouldn't dare, even if I could, Master," she said, ending her statement by biting her lip and staring lovingly at the dominant man. He grinned at her just before he disappeared from the bedroom for a few moments and she heard his car door close. A twinge of fear crept in her; she worried part of tonight's punishment was to leave her bound to the bed alone while he drove away, but when she heard the front door open again, she breathed a small sigh of relief.

Edgar came in with a grin on his face and a box in his hands. It wasn't very large, so at least it wasn't a monstrous dildo or some other horror like that, Skye reasoned. "You know, dear, I love spanking you, whipping you, paddling you and caning that ass of yours..." he said, letting his voice trail off.

"Yes, Master?" She felt her skin crawl with both fear and delicious anticipation.

"Sometimes, though, my arm gets a bit sore from it all. Not as sore as I make you, of course," he chuckled, "but I work with my hands all day, writing prescriptions, doing eye exams, and sometimes, our impact play sessions leave me sore the rest of the next day. Fret not, my dear, because I have a solution."

Edgar took out a small Swiss army knife from his pocket and cut the tape along the box. When he was finished, he pulled out a remote-control looking device with four white wires. Skye had watched enough porn with her husband to know what it was he bought, and her heart raced.

"Seven styles and fourteen settings of intensity for each," he read from the box's description. "Gentle massage, pulse, scratching, impact, steady, deep tissue, and random," he continued.

"Ooh," Skye said with both nervousness and desire. Her pussy was smoothly shaven, perfect to accept the pads which connected to the wires. They were similar to the type of gel pads hospitals used in EKG readings. Edgar plugged the adapter into the wall outlet and connected the wires to the device.

"Just think, Skye...I could go watch the game downstairs and come back when it's over. By then, you'll have had probably a few dozen orgasms, maybe even passed out. This is great!"

"Master, you...you wouldn't do that to me, would you?" she asked.

"You're right, I wouldn't. I enjoy watching you squirm too much to walk away from that. However, it does free my hands to do other things with you. While I'm zapping your clit, I could be fucking your ass, or if I'm shocking your thighs, I could even use that gorgeous mouth of yours to dump my load in you. Maybe I'll continue to whip you even as you're getting shocked."

Edgar saw her pussy open and close in response to the mere suggestion. Her toes curled and her eyes closed as she envisioned the idea. His wife was a bit of a pain slut. The more stimulation her body received, the better.

"Thank you, Master. This is an amazing gift," she said earnestly.

"Don't thank me just yet, sweetie. You might be cursing my name by the end of the evening."

"I'd *never* do that, my love," she vehemently denied. "No matter how much pain it might cause!"

"Where should we begin? I have four pads, four wires. Maybe...one on each inner thigh?" Edgar asked, then answered himself by placing the first two pads on her upper, inner-thighs, fairly close to her groin. Skye licked her lips in anticipation. "That leaves me two more. Hmm...I could slide them under your ass to give that gorgeous, pert butt of yours some attention, or...well...I think you know where I'm going to put them."

"Y-yes, Master," Skye stammered. She watched as he peeled away the protective plastic coating from the sticky gel pads. Her eyes grew wide as he placed the third pad on her fleshy labia lips, and the fourth directly on her clit hood. He was still fully dressed, and there was something so erotic to his wife seeing him in his dress slacks, shirt and tie while she was restrained to their bed naked, spread, and completely at his mercy.

Rather than turning the device on right away, he grabbed her breasts and started to play with them. He was rough but not out of control. He was *never* out of control. Control was everything to her master. Even when he came, he would merely grunt or sigh deeply as his hot stream of man gravy filled her mouth, ass or pussy. He kept his emotions in check, and it excited her when he fucked her with so little apparent emotion.

She was an empath. She could sense his love. Even if his face was as stern and cold as a blustery January dawn, Skye knew Edgar loved her deeply and passionately. She could read him like a book. The slightest change in his facial expression was like a neon sign for her. She could tell when he had a bad day by the tone of his voice, and she made it her mission to take his mind off of whatever was bothering him, usually by giving him incredible, passionate sex.

Edgar tugged on her erect nipples, twisting them between his thumbs and forefingers as he pulled. She yelped in pain and he held them in that position for a few seconds more before releasing them and watching them redden as the blood rushed back in. He grinned wickedly at her. "Basic physics, love. You know that electricity flows easily through liquids. Too bad for you that your pussy is so wet," he laughed.

"Please, Master, be gentle with me," she begged, but she fooled no one with those words.

"Now there's a lie. We both know that's not what you want. You can't wait for me to turn this on to maximum. You'll have to earn it, though. You'll have to pleasure me in order to receive your reward; the maximum setting. Are you ready, Baby Doll?”

"Yes, Master," she said, nodding her head.

"No, you're not. But it's going to happen either way," he said with a smirk.

Edgar turned on the device. No power entered the wires yet, but the beep and the glowing blue display startled Skye just the same. He placed his hand on her knee and tapped his fingers on it as he decided what to do next.

"I'll be right back," he assured her. A few minutes later, he returned with a pair of dice. "I'm not sure which mode or setting I should start off with, so I'll leave it up to the fates. There are fourteen settings, and the highest I can roll is a twelve, so thirteen and fourteen will be out of the question...for now."

"Yes, Master," she said dutifully.

"If, at any time, it gets too intense, your safe word is Albuquerque."

"I've never used a safe word yet," she said proudly.

"You know the punishment if you use it, right, doll face?" he asked, knowing how much she loved it when he spoke like a chauvinist from the middle of the last century.

"Deep throat blowjob, yes Master," she said, though she would do that for her lover regardless of whether or not it was a punishment.

"I love your gorgeous eyes, but I think...for tonight's games, you should be blindfolded," he said.

"Of course, Master," she said. The excitement was building for her, and she glanced at his groin, seeing a bulge against his slacks. It excited her knowing how much he wanted this, too.

He fetched a black, silk blindfold they had purchased together at a kinky toy shop. She was very used to wearing the blindfold, but not while having electricity course through her body. He tied it around the back of her head, and the silk made her world go dark. He watched her breathing quicken in pace. Her large, shapely breasts rose and fell rapidly with each breath. Her swollen, stiff nipples ached to be grabbed, but he focused on the task at hand.

He took the pair of dice and rolled it on her flat, taut belly. "A three and a one, that adds up to four. Let's see, impact. Well, lucky for you, that's nothing new." She heard him click the button which chirped four times until the proper mode was selected. "Now, to roll for the intensity setting," he said calmly. Once again, she heard him shake the dice in his hand and felt the cool cubes roll on her belly.

"Three and three, that's six," he proclaimed. He clicked the button until setting six was reached.

"Take a deep breath, darling," he said.

She breathed in, and as soon as she exhaled, he pressed the start button. Immediately, a stinging, snapping sensation was felt in both thighs, her labia and clit. It felt as if someone snapped a rubber band against each spot and managed to repeat the sensation every other second. Edgar watched with a smile on her face as her body involuntarily twitched with each pulse. They were small twitches, but noticeable. Her body began to bead with sweat, which would only aid with the conductivity of the devices. Skye yipped occasionally from the stinging shocks.

Skye breathed heavily in and out of her nose, making huffing, snorting sounds as the snapping sensation of the electricity struck her without end. Edgar slipped out of his shoes and socks, kicking them on the floor. He undid his tie and unbuttoned his shirt while his wife squirmed and huffed as the relentless tapping sensation tormented some of the most sensitive parts of her body. He shimmied out of his pants and tossed off his boxers.

"How's it feeling, babe?" he asked.

"I can handle it, Master," she replied with labored breath.

He turned it up to eight. "How about now?"

Her toes splayed and her fingers clenched into fists. She bit her lip and smiled. "It feels good, Master," she groaned and then jerked again as new bolts punished those sensitive spots.

"There's another setting I didn't tell you about. Not only can I control the intensity of the shock, but also the speed of the intervals between them. Observe," he said, and she felt the tapping sensation speed up. He also dialed up the intensity to setting nine while he was at it.

"Oh..." she moaned and wriggled against her steel bindings.

"That's my girl," he cooed happily.

"More, please, Master," she begged.

"Oh, what a cheeky little brat," he chuckled. He skipped about four settings higher and Skye yelped with pleasure and pain. She shuddered and shivered, and her pussy was dripping like a leaky faucet moistening the bedsheet. Without warning, Edgar set the knob to maximum power.

"Oh, oh, umph, oh f-fuck!" she moaned and cried. Her body literally rippled with each jolt of the device. It was interesting watching how her body reacted differently to each level. Edgar began stroking his cock intermittently while watching his wife writhe. When she had been punished enough, Edgar switched over to a massage mode at a much gentler setting and speed.

Still huffing and breathing through her teeth from the first session, it took Skye a moment to realize the sensations were no longer painful but rather pleasant. It felt like a vibrator sending waves of delirious sensations deep into her vaginal walls, her labia, her clit. Edgar got off the bed to fetch a more familiar toy; his black, leather riding crop. When he returned, she flinched when the riding crop traced over her nude body from her chin down to her toes. He began lightly smacking her smooth thighs with the crop, leaving gentle pink marks where the leather impacted.

"You didn't think I'd let you enjoy that setting without there being a price to pay, did you?" he asked.

"No, Master," she replied breathlessly.

Her fair, pale skin was the perfect canvass to be marked. While the electricity gently stimulated her, he increased the intensity of his whipping.

He rolled the dice again: "looks like you're going to get the random setting," he announced, then rolled again for the intensity level. "Ooh, two sixes, you're going to get setting twelve right off the bat," he chuckled. Edgar adjusted the device accordingly and pressed the start button.

There was a bit of a pause, then he watched sky's back arch as a jolt of power stimulated her labia, clit and thighs. He began whipping her legs yet again, but this time, with full gusto. The random effects and delays between shocks were slightly terrifying to Skye, but thrilling nonetheless. Her husband's expert use of the crop only added to the experience. Skye writhed and jolted, shivered and splayed, groaned, yipped, laughed and screamed, all depending on what setting the device randomly chose.

Edgar positioned himself at her side and began striking her perfect breasts with the thin whip. Sky almost started to say "Alb..." for the safe word, but caught herself.

"Do you want me to stop?" he asked.

"No, Master," she said bravely.

"Good girl," he cooed, and began smacking her breasts once again. He watched beads of sweat appear all over her nude, bound body. The relentless zapping never let up in intensity, nor did her husband with his crop. When he decided she had enough punishment, he turned off the machine and removed the gel pads, but kept her bound and blindfolded. There were still several settings left unexplored, but uncharacteristically for a man so in-control, he found himself lusting to plow his wife.

She heard him tearing open a condom package and knew what was coming next. Edgar knelt behind his wife's spread legs and rubbed his cock against her smoothly shaven, recently abused pussy. It was dripping with her desire and still twitched from phantom pulses of electricity her mind imagined were occurring. He unceremoniously entered her tight pussy and rammed his long, thick cock deep inside her.

"Oh, Master," she gasped. "Yes!"

"You took those settings like a champ, my love. Time to get your reward!"

"Mm, thank you, Master!" she cooed deliriously.

Edgar wrapped his muscular, right arm around her neck and gently squeezed as he rammed his rod into her willing sex. The splashing, smacking noise of his thighs impacting hers, his cock ravishing her drenched pussy, now filled the air. With his left hand, he fondled her large, shapely breasts, roughly squeezing them, pulling on her nipples.

He loosened his grip on her neck and put the palm of his hand against her mouth. She licked it seductively all while happily cooing and squealing. She was very familiar with the feeling of his hard meat rod invading her deep, tight tunnel and relished every time he fucked her like a buck in heat. Edgar pulled out before he got too far along. He undid her ankle shackles and lifted her legs to rest on his shoulders, then spread her butt cheeks wide.

"You know what's coming next, don't you, baby?" he asked.

"Yes, Master," she said dreamily.

"Beg for it. I want to hear my Baby Girl ask nicely."

"Please, Master...fuck my ass. Fuck it hard. Fuck the naughty out of me!"

"You can do better," he said with a grin.

"Please, Master! Fuck me like a piece of meat. I need your huge cock in my ass! Please..."

"That's my girl," he said, and he spit in her tight star and slid his massive cock in, inch by inch.

Skye still wasn't used to getting pounded in the ass, but she loved pleasing her master, so she breathed deeply and relaxed as much as she could while he drove deeper down inside. Edgar loved the tight feeling of her ass and grunted with satisfaction. He began slowly thrusting his fuck stick back and forth against her tight little star.

"Oh, oh yes," she whimpered nasally. Every time he fucked her ass, it felt a little better than the last, and she knew she would eventually crave it like every other wicked thing they did together.

Edgar began spanking the ass he was fucking, grabbing it harshly after each swat. The pain was deliriously good for her and she felt a powerful orgasm coming.

"Please, sir...cum inside me, please," she practically cried.

"I will, Baby Doll, don't you worry about that," he said. He pulled her hair back, making her head tilt backwards as he smacked his balls against her ass. He positioned himself on one knee has he furiously pumped her ass and began fingering her pussy hard.

"M-master, can I please, can I please cum?" she begged as he pounded her with fury.

"Not yet, baby. Hold on just a little more," he said between gritted teeth. Skye couldn't even reply as she used every ounce of her strength to fight off the inexorable orgasm encroaching.

He increased his tempo as fast as he could pound her, and he felt his balls tightening as he was ready to release. "Now. Cum for me now!" he suddenly ordered. His voice was so booming and demanding, there was nothing she could do but comply.

It was the command she had been waiting for, and a flood of endorphins racked her brain as her belly felt hot, her legs felt like jelly and her pussy felt as electric as when the pads were coursing juice through her. Even with her blindfold on, she could see her lover's reaction in her mind's eye as he growled when he released.

Edgar felt the surge of hot cum race from his balls out his steel-hard dick. The condom filled with his salty gravy and her ass was thoroughly violated by the time he blew his load into the rubber. He pulled out a few seconds later staring at the gaping hole from his thick cock which he left in his wife's conquered ass. Both were panting, sweating, gasping for air. He kissed one of the red marks on her breast gently and unlocked her bindings.

He undid her blindfold and kissed her passionately. Skye wrapped her arms around his naked, ripped body and looked at her master dreamily. "You know, honey, there are still several settings we didn't explore on your new little toy," she said saucily.

"In due time, my princess. In due time. Now, I believe you still owe me a foot rub," he said with a wicked grin. Her eyes seemed to sparkle at the suggestion and she nearly pounced on his legs as she went to work adoring his bare feet.

To most of the outside world, their relationship would be considered strange, kinky, and harken back to a bygone era generally eschewed by modern society. Luckily for Edgar and Skyler, they answered only to each other. Behind those closed doors was the happiest couple one could ever meet, and the love they had for each other only grew with each increasingly dramatic romp in the bedroom.

Story 2: Forever Home

Jim Mullins was never what one might call a "social butterfly." The thirty-one-year-old web developer was proudly introverted, happily misanthropic, and intensely private. The developer was classified in the Myers-Briggs test as a relatively rare INTJ: an Introverted, Intuitive, Thinking, Judging type. So, it came as an utter shock to his one close friend, Angelo, when he learned the recluse was advertising for a roommate for his spacious condo.

"I don't get it, dude," Angelo said. "Aren't you a proud INTJ, one of those reclusive misanthropes who hates society and wants humanity to fuck off into oblivion?" he asked, scratching his head.

"Yeah, so?" Jim countered blandly.

"Looking for a roommate just doesn't seem...you," his friend said.

"It isn't; but money talks, and if I don't find a roommate to help foot the bill, I'll have to walk. My landlord is such a douche, but that place is everything I've ever dreamed of."

"Yeah, I know you really do love that condo," Angelo said. "Most people have pictures of their family or dogs at their work desks; you have a picture of your gaming station."

"Again, I ask: yeah, so? Hopefully, it's just temporary until I can get a raise from work or someone investigates the landlord for being a douche."

"You'll be kicking your roomie out eventually?" Angelo asked.

"By then, I'm pretty sure they'll be looking for any and all excuses to get the fuck away from me," he chuckled.

"Yeah," Angelo agreed then quickly added "uh, I mean, I'm sure you'll get the raise...or something."

The first week of interviewing potential candidates went horribly wrong for Jim. Most were put-off by his dark demeanor, lack of smiles, black ensemble, and drab, minimalist décor. The others were off-putting to Jim; party animals, rambunctious, vapid and annoying. Then, on the second week, he met Julie.

"Wow, this is a nice place," she said as soon as she stepped into the condo.

"Thanks," Jim said, somewhat surprised by her reaction.

"Are those Star Trek figures? Fucking awesome!" she said, noticing the figures almost as soon as she entered the room.

"You're a Trekkie?" he asked.

"Is a Ferengi a good businessman?" she countered. He chuckled too quietly to be heard, or at least he thought so.

"You have a cute smile!" she said, unapologetically and without any reservation.

"Uh, anyway...tell me some things about you," he recovered from the unexpected compliment.

"Well, I'm twenty-five, a bit of a bookworm; I hope you don't mind me sitting quietly in the corner while I read."

"No, not at all," he said honestly. "I'm a bit of a bookworm myself," he admitted.

"Oh? What genres?" Julie prodded.

"Historical fiction, sci-fi, alternative history," he said softly.

Julie shuffled around in her purse and produced her Kindle book reader. "Here; take a look at *this* library," she said with a confident smile.

"Whoa, you've got good taste in authors," he said, then cleared his throat and tried to sound more like his normal standoffish self. "I mean, interesting selection." He was happy with that; he didn't want to seem too eager around her.

"I tend to be a good judge of literature, along with people," she said with a warm smile. There was something infectious about her smile. It seemed to sear into his soul, and it almost made him uncomfortable, but at the same time, yearning for more. He loved it, but hated it. He secretly wanted no roommate at all and just go back to the way things were, but the cost of rent was too high, and he settled for trying to find the least annoying candidate. By least annoying, his heart was saying "beautiful," because that's what his emotions were telling him as he stared at her.

Her hair was dark and wavy, giving her an exotic, almost gypsy-like appeal, yet her eyes were green like emeralds and intoxicating for him to stare at. Jim had a hard time concentrating on the conversation; a very rare occurrence for the normally stoic man, but her charm, beauty, and bubbly personality made him lose a bit of his icy self-control.

"When can you move in?" Jim blurted out.   The question caught her off-guard, because she was still expecting more in-depth interview questions.

"Uh…as early as this week," she said. "Does this mean…?"

"It's yours if you want it. I'll give you a good deal on the rate," he said. He actually bit his tongue until it hurt. He couldn't believe how much like a slobbering puppy he just sounded like to her.

She shocked him when she practically pounced on the dark-haired, dark-eyed, bespectacled man and hugged him tightly. "Sorry," she said immediately after doing so. "I'm…just super-duper excited!"

"I can see that," he said with a dry chuckle, but his face turned flush.

"I can't wait to move in. I promise, you won't regret it!" Julie said cheerily, but the nagging self-doubts assailing the overanalytical thinker already made him wonder if he already regretted the decision.

By Friday that week, she had moved her possessions over to the condo. Her tastes were a bit eclectic, colorful, and eccentric, and if it had been anyone else, Jim would have probably been annoyed with the little personal touches she added to his dark, dreary dwelling. He found himself annoyed with how easily he bent to her good-natured demands and desires. Was this the same Jim Mullins who voted for a giant asteroid to end humanity in the last election? He felt almost queasy as he thought about it, but then took a deep breath and tried to regain a sense of composure and control.

"Just a few ground rules, though," Jim said as Julie was helping herself to an apple. She listened while taking a bite. "I'm...a pretty reserved, quiet, introverted and private person. I need my personal space, so if I'm locked in my room, please understand it's nothing personal, it's just me and I really need it."

"Totally get that," she said, taking another bite. "I can be the exact same way!"

"Uh, that's good; also, I'll respect your privacy. If you're bringing your boyfriend over, just let me know, I'll disappear in my room and you won't even know I exist. Don't even worry about me for a second; I'll be fine in there."

"Oh, I don't have a boyfriend," she was quick to add.

"Uh...girlfriend?" he said.

"No, silly," she laughed. "I'm single," she said and began singing *One is the Loneliest Number*. He interrupted her singing.

"Oh...okay. Well, I'm sure that won't last forever, so when you do bring someone home, I'll stay out of your hair."

"I appreciate that," she said. "And I'll do the same for you."

"Oh, I'm...uh...not relationship material," he chuckled nervously. "So, I don't think that will be much of an issue."

"Not relationship material?" she asked with genuine confusion.

"Yeah."

"Why do you say that?"

"I'm shy, aloof, nerdy, reclusive, and far from attractive."

She smiled wryly and said "not every girl is into buff, alpha-macho, meathead types. I'm sure you're just being too hard on yourself."

"Yeah, perhaps, but....never mind," he said, trying to drop the subject, but she noticed he turned red again. "Um, how do you want to handle meals? Everyone on their own, or take turns cooking and doing dishes?"

"Well, if we'd always be on our own for food, you'd never get to try my famous lemon-piccata chicken, or my five-alarm chili," she said with a wink.

"Alright, so every other day we take turns cooking, and the one who doesn't cook does dishes?"

"Seems fair," she said.

"Great, looks like we figured that out," he said nervously, and she grinned at his awkwardness. She found his dark, quirky demeanor to be charming when others ran the other way. Though she was much better at hiding it, she felt just as awkward around this handsome man who didn't seem to see what she saw in him.

Over the next few months, things settled down for the two. They got to know each other over time, and they enjoyed having deep discussions almost every night. The awkwardness all but evaporated between the two, and they felt like best friends, perhaps even soulmates. Jim felt like he had a girlfriend without having a girlfriend. It was shocking how easily he let his guard down when talking with her.

For her part, Julie loved having someone listen so attentively to her rambling stories. Other people would tell her to shut up or to stay focused on one topic, but Jim seemed to have no problem keeping up with her chaotic story-telling and even rehashing the story in a way that made logical sense...which often shocked her.

Julie eventually revealed to Jim her Myers-Briggs type was an ENFP, or extroverted, intuitive, feeling and perceiving. Though three of the four functions were polar opposites to Jim's their shared intuitive styles made their connection run deeper than either was prepared for. Julie felt like someone finally, completely, truly understood her. No one; not former lovers, best friends or even family seemed to have this same almost mystical bond like he seemed to share with her. She was also impressed at how caring, thoughtful, and open this self-described misanthropic recluse really was. She definitely saw him act like that to other people, but around her, he was sweet, gentle, excited and attentive.

They discussed everything from conspiracy theories to fiction genres, watched Netflix movies together, and even played board games and video games together. Few people got to see his gaming pride and joy, fewer still were allowed to play the games, but he didn't mind sharing his game setup with her.

It took some time, but it was Julie who decided they were in a relationship, whether he knew it or not. They were doing everything couples would do, except for one rather important part. So, she decided to coyly start hinting at it and bringing things up to *encourage* the shy man in the right direction. She was a very sexual person; sex was an integral part of her life, but she craved to have it with someone she could connect with on an emotional, intellectual, and even spiritual level. Physical sex with former partners was satisfying, but it always left her feeling strangely vacant, missing something.

The ENFP started to fantasize about Jim. She started to become very touchy and feely with him, brushing his arm when she'd hand him something, bumping her foot against his as they ate their meals, sitting closer to him than necessary when watching TV or playing games. What became maddening to Julie was how oblivious he was to it all. She knew this man was no ordinary person, and she would have to ramp up her efforts dramatically to get him in bed with her.

Julie was sneaky with her subtle manipulations and her plan to bed the man was no exception. She picked the Netflix movie that evening and it was one she had seen before. There were several steamy, sexy scenes in the film, which gave her the opportunity to start planting ideas in his head. When the two main characters where in bed fucking their brains out, Julie commented "man, it's been too long."

"Too long?" he asked, oblivious as always to her subtle flirting.

"Oh, since I did something like that," she chuckled innocently, but not too innocently.

"Ah," he replied. "Well, that's probably because you spend all this time hanging around me instead of finding someone to do that with."

A slight smirk crept on her lips. "That's *very* true," she said.

He paused the movie. "You should change that. I'm serious. Julie, you're an amazing person; very attractive, bubbly, kind, intelligent, and vivacious. You shouldn't be sitting at home watching Netflix with me. You should be Netflix and chilling with someone."

"That's also *very true*," she giggled.

"Look, don't make my mistake. Don't be like me. If you find someone you have the hots for, you go for it, and don't worry about me."

"Advice taken, but I'll always worry about you," she said.

"Nah, don't do that. I'm fine," he said with a slightly pained, forced smile. She thought it was sweet how he wanted her to be happy, and even sweeter how he didn't realize she didn't have to look too far to find that happiness.

"And what about you? What about your needs?"

"Like I said," he chuckled, "don't worry about me."

"But I do. I want you to be able to...Netflix and chill...too," she said.

"I'm fine...just...don't barge in my room after eleven, if you get my meaning," he chuckled and then turned red after he realized what he said. Of course, for Julie, when someone would tell her not to do something, it was the first thing she wanted to x. do. "I mean...never mind, just let's watch the movie."

Julie figured as much about him, but to get him to admit as much didn't gross her out or make her laugh at him. She just felt that his hand should take a break from pleasuring himself and that he should let her do it for him.

"Sorry to make things awkward," he said, turning red.

She laughed softly. "I was the one who brought it up, remember? Besides, I didn't find it awkward at all. You're a human being with needs. We *all are*," she dropped another subtle clue that was never picked up.

"Yeah, but I didn't have to go there," he said, still apologizing.

"Maybe I'm glad you did. We talk about everything *except* that," she replied.

"Well, I don't want things to get weird," he said.

"Jim, all of our conversations have been weird. What about the UFOs killed Kennedy conspiracy?" Julie said with a laugh. She grabbed the remote and paused the movie this time. "Come on, you tell me your most embarrassing sex story, and I'll tell you mine."

"I don't want to," he said grumpily.

"Oh, come on, it can't be *that* embarrassing," she prodded.

"Let's just watch the movie," he begged.

"Alright, but if you won't share yours, I'll at least share mine. So, back in college, I was with this guy, Jack McPherson. So, we're in the drive-thru of the Wendy's and as he's giving out the order through the speaker, I decided it would be a good time to give him a hand-job. I unbuckled and unzipped his pants, and he's like 'what are you doing, Julie?' and I'm like, 'I want to try your Frosty.' So, we're waiting for the food to come out and I'm jerking his dick under his jacket I put over his lap. Well, I must've done a pretty good job, because he suddenly lurches forward on the gas and rear-ends a Volvo in front of us. You should have seen how pissed off the lady driving in front of us was. I felt so bad, I probably ruined his insurance rate, and he never did get to climax. He dumped me the next day."

Jim chuckled at that and shook his head. "You're truly certifiable," he said.

"Oh, I know it." She stared at the paused TV for a moment and then said "come on, tell me yours!"

"No!" he protested.

"Why not? It can't be any worse than mine," she teased.

"I don't have one," he said bitterly.

"None of your sexual adventures were ever embarrassing? You're that much of a straight-shooter?"

"No, because I never *had one*," he said. There was an awkward silence as they stared at the frozen TV set for a moment before Jim got up and went to his room.

Julie was not expecting that, and her plan backfired spectacularly. She went from trying to seduce him to having to go into immediate damage control. Jim locked the door and she tried rattling the door knob. She knocked. "Come on, Jim. Let me in."

"No," he replied.

"I'm sorry. I was being totally insensitive. I had no idea."

"I don't want to talk about it," she heard his muffled reply through the door.

"Well, I do. There's nothing to be ashamed about, Jim. I just assumed a handsome man like you had already several experiences."

"Well, I didn't, alright?"

"I'm sorry, Jim…I never wanted to hurt your feelings."

"It's alright, I'm fine, go away now," he said.

She knew he needed space, and she gave it to him. Julie went back to her room to masturbate in frustration, but all the porn in the world couldn't replace the image of her taking this handsome but shy and aloof man's virginity. What started as a project would now become a mission.

Over the next week, their interactions were beyond awkward. They'd make and eat dinner without so much as making eye-contact. Conversations were kept to bare minimums. The lack of deep conversations was driving Julie mad, and after a solid week had gone by with Jim retreating to his room shortly after the dishes were cleaned, she had enough. She couldn't possibly have sex with him if he would be in this never-ending loop of his.

"Jim, we need to talk," she said, but he retreated to his room once more.

The locks on the interior doors were pathetic; a simple toothpick poked in the hole in the knob was enough to unlock them, and Julie finally found one. Reasoning with him through the door was impossible. She wanted to speak with him face-to-face. She poked the hole in the door with the toothpick and barged in.

To her shock, Jim's pants were already down to his ankles, along with his underwear. His laptop rested on his chest and he had his hand on his cock as he was jerking to what was clearly a dominatrix leading her male slave by a leash. "Holy shit! What the fuck are you doing here?" Jim asked, slamming the laptop shut.

"Sorry, I...I just wanted to talk and...oh my," she saw his cock in its semi-hard stage and got a good glimpse of it before he covered it up with his blanket.

"Get out!" he screamed.

She quickly closed the door behind her, but the image of his cock in his hand still stuck with her. She went back to her room and was breathing heavily out of fear. She worried he would have her move out of the condo the next morning and she started to cry. Even with her eyes closed from crying, she saw his dick, and she couldn't help but start fantasizing about him. The brief glimpse at his porn of choice meshed very well with her own sexuality.

Though Julie kept it hidden well, she had quite a dominant streak in her. She pictured herself as the dominatrix in the video, leading a naked Jim by the leash. She'd then have him lay on his back as she grabbed the leash and pinned him to the floor, fucking him as she rode on him, rocking her hips back and forth. Her fingers reached down to her pants and she slid them under her panties and started to masturbate to thoughts of dominating this delicious introvert.

The next morning was a Saturday and Jim was just finishing his breakfast when Julie entered the kitchen. "Julie, we need to talk."

"Yes, we do," she agreed.

"Last night, you broke one of the few cardinal rules I have here. I've been pretty tolerant when you leave your tooth brush on the sink or when you forget to put the creamer back in the fridge, but last night you went too far. I'm...I hate the fact I have to do this, but I'm going to have to ask you to find another place. You can stay until you find one, but I want you to leave as soon as possible."

"No," she said simply. There wasn't defiance or malice in her voice; it was a simple reply.

"No? What do you mean no? I'm terminating your contract," he said.

"No," she said nonchalantly as she began fixing herself some coffee.

"Listen, I don't know who you think you are, but…"

She approached him as he sat at the table and stood in front of him. "I *know* who I am, Jim. And you're going to find out, too." Julie felt her heart beating fast. She was taking a risk, but desperate times called for desperate measures.

"What the hell are you talking about?" he demanded.

"I saw enough of what you're into on that laptop of yours, but guess what?" she bent down and whispered in his ear "*I am too.*"

"You're what?" he asked nervously. Julie went back to the coffee pot to add water.

"I know I may not *look* it, Jim, but there's a serious dominant streak in me. I have a type I'm attracted to. Shy, intellectual, nerdy, submissive boys with dark hair and dark eyes," she said in her most sultry voice. She approached him once again. "Let me give you what you want…what you *need*. Let me have what *I want and need.*"

"You're full of shit, this is crazy," he said dismissively, but she detected a great deal of uncertainty in the wavering in his voice.

"Oh sweetie, we haven't even gotten close to crazy yet," she said, running her fingers up his arm and added "crazy is when I'm pegging you with a strap-on, and I'm pulling on your nipple clamps with my teeth."

"Stop, I know what you're doing, and it's not going to work."

"What am I doing?" she asked innocently.

"You feel bad that I'm a virgin, you felt bad for barging in last night, so you're trying to seduce me to make me feel better. And you're trying to keep from getting kicked out!"

"Well, you're right about the seducing part," she laughed.

"Come on, stop playing with me. You aren't attracted to me," he said getting up to wash his coffee mug, but as he did, the shorter woman managed to pin him against the kitchen wall. "What are you doing?" he demanded, but she was stronger than her height and stature let on.

"No one tells me who I am and am not attracted to. Now, if you're not attracted to me, I'll respect that, and I'll pack my things and leave. But...something tells me I'm not wrong, that you *do* find me attractive."

He was quiet for a moment as she still pinned him gently against the wall. "You are attractive," he begrudgingly admitted.

"And I find *you* attractive. Why do you think I touch you every chance I get? Why did I make us watch that raunchy movie last week? Why do you think I add as much inuendo in our conversations as possible? I've wanted to bang you since the moment I laid my eyes on you...and when I saw that cock of yours last night. Mm. So, what say we stop all this yelling and start doing things that are a whole lot more enjoyable?"

"Why?" he asked.

"Because I'd rather fuck than fight," she replied.

"No, I mean *why* would you find me attractive?" he asked with genuine puzzlement.

"Well, I'll give you the abridged version because I don't want to spend the entire weekend listing all the reasons, even though I could. You're smart, and I have a thing for brainy people. You're actually way more handsome than you give yourself credit; your hair is dark and clean cut, your eyes are piercing when you're lost in thought, and...well I've already seen a glimpse of another...ahem...asset you possess. Beyond that, you're always kind to me, caring, sweet and gentle, we have the most amazing conversations, and aside from this little incident, we never fight. Plus, I wasn't lying when I said I'm sexually dominant. Do you know how hard it is to find a good looking, smart, sophisticated submissive man?"

"This is all a bit much to take in," he said, sitting down after he put the cup away.

"You'll be saying that when we try pegging for the first time," she said lightly.

He put his head in his hands and thought for a while. Julie took the chair and moved it over to sit next to him. She put her hands on his back and started to massage him gently. "I can see I can't get rid of you that easily," he said.

"Nope," she replied and began kneading him more forcefully.

"Fuck, that feels nice," he admitted.

"I want you to feel a whole lot more than just nice," she said.

"I can't believe any of this is happening," he said.

"Neither can I," she admitted with a nervous smile. "But I want it to happen."

"You...really are dominant?" he asked.

"Come to my room, I want to show you something," she said. He had never really been in her bedroom since she moved in, much in the same way Julie never went into Jim's until that fateful night. When he entered, he saw lots of colorful decorations. Pinks, purples, oranges and yellows assaulted his eyes. He half-expected a sex-slave dungeon based on how she built up the reveal to him. She turned on her flower-sticker-bedazzled laptop and opened a folder to show him an absolute plethora of female domination videos and pictures.

"Holy crap," he remarked.

"Uh-huh," she admitted.

"I think that's more than *I've* got," he chuckled.

"What can I say? I have a high libido," she giggled. "Pics and vids are all fine and good, but they're no substitute for the real thing," she said, having him sit down on his bed. "I've got lots of...toys," she pulled a box of sex toys from under her bed. Jim's eyes widened when he saw everything from dildos to handcuffs, riding crops, cat-o-nine tail whips, and so many more naughty toys.

"Oh shit," he gasped.

"Look, Jim, I want you to know, I respect and love you. I would not do anything to intentionally hurt you, and if we do play with these toys, I'll have your consent and full knowledge. I won't blindfold you and then peg you with a giant, fourteen-inch dildo if it would not be something you'd want."

"Well...fourteen might be a tad much," he chuckled nervously.

"Noted; the Ass-Blaster 5,000 will not make an appearance," she said with a smarmy smile. He chuckled again.

"Glad we got that straightened out," he said.

"Jim..."

"Yes, Julie?"

"Is it alright if I kiss you now?" she asked.

Jim paused for an awkward moment, then slowly nodded. He felt the air suddenly get heavy and heard the thump of his own heartbeat in his ears as the blood rushed to his head. This beautiful woman, with whom he had spent the past few months living with, now tilted her head slightly, closed her eyes, and a hint of a smile appeared on her lips before they met with his. Her lips were soft, warm and slightly moist. The kiss was everything either one of them could hope for.

Julie's hands began caressing Jim's back. She snaked her hands lower until she found the bottom of his t-shirt, then pulled it up over his head, barely breaking the kiss to do so. Jim wasn't ripped with muscles defining his abs or pecs, but his belly was relatively flat and his chest smooth. Julie's hands had to explore his chest. She loved how smooth it felt, knowing her tongue certainly explore him as well. Her fingers found his nipples and she rubbed them gently until they hardened, then gave them gentle tugs which grew stronger and more aggressive with each passing second.

"Ah!" he exclaimed.

Julie giggled. "What? I *told* you I'm dominant. Did you think I was kidding? Lay down on your back on my bed."

"Julie...I don't have a condom," he admitted.

"Do you think your mistress would be so unprepared?" she laughed and produced a box with multiple sizes to find out which one was best for him. "But don't worry, we haven't quite gotten to that part, yet. I want to have some more fun with you, first."

She unbuckled his belt, unbuttoned and unzipped his pants, undid his shoes and slipped off his socks. Within a matter of minutes, Jim was lying naked on his roommate's bed. She produced a pair of pink, fuzzy handcuffs and slid them between the railing of her headboard. "Give me your wrists," she demanded softly but firmly. Without even thinking, Jim complied. He felt the soft cuffs attach to his wrists and he was now bound and unable to escape. She produced a pair of similar fuzzy shackles for his ankles and attached them to the footboard and then his feet. If he had any doubts that she was dominant before, they evaporated now.

"I just want to stand back and stare at you. Look at you, the strong, silent type, all stoic and morose every day, now you're bound to my bed in pretty, pink cuffs, completely at my mercy." Jim wondered if he had just made a mistake and she saw the look of doubt in his eyes.

"You look nervous, honey. Do I make you nervous?" she giggled. "Does little Julie make the big, mean, Jim frightful?"

"Maybe...a little," he admitted.

"Aww, well don't you worry about a thing. Mistress will take good care of you. I know you better than you think. I know what you want and what you need. You might think you need a cruel mistress to treat you like trash, to humiliate you, to torture you mercilessly. I can tell that's not what you really need, though. You need a soft, loving mistress who will guide you, correct you, and give you the compassionate love you deserve."

"I do?" he asked.

"Mistress knows best," she giggled. "Now, I've seen you naked, I think it's only fair if I reciprocate," she said. Julie slipped out of her shoes and slid her shirt off. Her blue bra held back luscious, pear-shaped breasts that were large but just right for Jim. Julie climbed on to his nude body and pressed her breasts against his face.

"I've seen you sneak more than one glance at them. Do you like what you see?" she asked.

Dumbfounded, Jim could only nod with his mouth slightly agape. Julie grinned and took the opportunity to put her nipple in his open mouth. Her soft, warm nipple touched his lips and it was almost a shock to the still stunned man. He gently kissed it.

"You can do more than just kiss them," she said softly. "Go on, taste them," she offered. Hesitantly, he began to suckle on her erect nipples as she alternated which one would be in his mouth. He explored the fleshy nubbins, rolling them with his tongue. She cradled his head in her hands as he adored her nipples with his mouth and let out a satisfied moan. "Yeah, just like that, baby," she cooed.

"Wow," Jim gasped as he reluctantly let go of the most perfect thing to ever enter his mouth. Julie shifted position to give her other nipple to her captive audience. Once again, he lovingly tasted, teased, and titillated his mistress's nipple. She kept switching between the left and right breast, massaging them as he suckled. When she was done, she playfully rubbed her tits in his face and laughed as she did so.

"That wasn't even close to wow. But don't you worry; wow is yet to…come…" she said with a wink. Julie unbuckled her belt and undid her jeans, sliding them off her legs and kicking them off the bed. Now, only her black lace panties provided her any form of clothing. Jim looked down at them and the back up at Julie's eyes. She crawled back up on his nude body and rubbed her panty-clad pussy against his raging boner and cooed gently.

"Oh fuck," he groaned softly, sounding almost as if in pain.

"Soon enough, love, soon enough," Julie replied. She hooked her thumbs in the elastic band of her panties and began slowly working them down. Her beautiful, cleanly shaven pussy was now revealed to the awkward, nerdy man. He thought it a minor miracle how he didn't cum at the sight.

As if reading his mind, she winked playfully and said "don't cum yet, sweetheart. If you do, you'll be punished!" To further tease him, she nestled his cock against her butt cheeks and ran her booty up and down along the length of his shaft. Jim whimpered while she giggled. The gorgeous woman leaned in close and kissed his lips once again.

There was something different in this kiss; it was more passionate, slower, more exploratory, more sensual. She closed her eyes for a moment then opened them again and locked her gaze with his. She smiled with her eyes while her hands explored his neck, back and shoulders. Jim wished he could return the favor, but he was bound securely and could only receive her touch, not give it back.

Positioning herself now to place her smooth pussy in her face, she looked down at her captive lover and gave the sultriest smile imaginable. "Would you like to taste me?" she asked. He nodded. "Would you really, now?" she continued.

"Yes, please," he said.

"Beg for it."

"Please, Julie, let me taste your pussy," he practically whined.

"Good boy," she replied, shuffling her hand through his hair approvingly. She spread her labia lips wide, letting him drink in her feminine scent for a moment. Her pink sex was glistening, begging to be licked; as much as he was hard, she was wet. Closer she moved until he was able to taste her for the first time.

Jim couldn't believe how sweet she tasted, like ripe honeydew melon; fresh, soft, juicy. Julie cooed softly as his tongue began to greedily explore the folds in her labia. He dipped his tongue in, fucking her gently with just his tongue. The surprising move sent shivers down the woman's back and she began kneading his hair in her fists, grabbing on and tugging at it gently.

"Oh, Jim," she whispered.   Jim then found her clit.

Everything he had done with his tongue before paled in comparison. When the tip of his tongue wiggled over the little bundle of nerves, Julie practically screamed with joy. Her extreme reaction momentarily startled Jim, but he recovered and redoubled his efforts, wiggling over her clitoris as fast as his tongue would allow. She began leaking her juices on his chin, the sweet nectar filling his tongue with sinful bliss. She was getting close. Too close. Much as she hated the idea, she pulled away.

"What?" Jim protested vehemently.

"Time for a little more fun, my dear," she said deviously and found some toys to play with.   The first device she selected was a Wartenberg pinwheel. The metal device looked like the spur on a cowboy boot attached to a little metal handle. The spikey pinwheel looked wicked to Jim and his eyes widened with terror.

"W-what's that?" he asked.

"A Wartenberg pinwheel; each little spike will leave an unpleasant little sensation as I glide it over your beautiful skin. We've known each other for months. Do you trust me, Jim?" Julie asked.

The   INTJ   nerdy   stud   nodded apprehensively.   Julie smiled warmly and straddled her naked body on his abdomen. She looked down at the bound man and slowly spun the wheel with her finger. "Ooh," she winced, making him all the more nervous.

Julie started with his outstretched right arm, traveling from his wrist to his sensitive armpits. The sensation of the sharp, little pins gently poking him felt like little needles grazing him. It wasn't agonizing, but it was far from pleasant. The lower she went down his arm, the closer she got to his armpit, and he jerked when she finally reached it.

"My, my; are we ticklish?" she asked, wiggling her finger over his armpit. He burst out laughing and struggled vainly to get away from her tormenting fingers. "Yes, we most certainly are!" she cooed.

"Please, no!" he begged.

"Don't worry, honey, I won't tickle you too much tonight. We have lots of time to explore together. I want to see how you react to Mr. Prickly traveling down your naked body," Julie said saucily and began gently, carefully running the sharp instrument down the sides of his neck. He closed his eyes, trying to remain perfectly still, but the strange sensations made him whimper slightly.

"Don't..." he begged.

"Don't what?" she asked.

"Don't make me bleed there!" he said frantically.

"Sweetie, I would *never*. The only thing I want oozing from you tonight is your delicious cum."

With that, Julie traced the pinwheel down his chest, making certain to pay extra special attention to his sensitive nipples with the cruel device. Jim was breathing through his teeth and trying to stay as still as he could manage. Her pinwheel mercifully left his nipples to explore his flat belly. He winced when she drove it gently into his bellybutton.

"You're being such a good boy for me," Julie said, licking her lips with satisfaction.

"Thank you, Mistress," he blurted out, and his face immediately turned red from the embarrassing utterance. She stroked his cheeks gently with her fingers and looked lovingly into his eyes. "You're very welcome, my grumpy little angel."

Her little wheel of pleasure and pain avoided his groin but definitely explored his thighs, causing him to jump with each stroke, then his shins, and she finally ended on the soles of his feet, causing him to once again burst out into laughter. "You are very, *very* ticklish. Just how I like it."

"Please, Mistress, my balls are aching, let me cum," he begged. She grinned again and kissed his forehead gently.

"We're going to finish together, and you're going to be inside me," she said matter-of-factly.

Fetching the right sized condom, she hurriedly opened it and slipped it on his throbbing, aching cock. She turned so she could look him in the eye as she lowered her waiting sex over his.

"Are you ready?" she asked. He nodded emphatically. With a small grin, she lowered herself over him, taking his cock in and taking his virginity. Julie marveled at the size of his long, thick, iron-hard rod as she let him enter bit by bit. She felt every twitch of his staff inside her sensitive, tight pussy and groaned with bliss.

Jim never would have thought he would have lost his virginity to his roommate/best friend, much less spread-eagle bound to her bed, after begging to eat the woman out and being slowly tortured by her pizza cutter from Hell, but at the same time, this was better than any of the scenarios he imagined. Her hot pussy enveloped his cock, lowering down, down, down, taking all of him in. He gasped and then gasped again as her fingers fondled and pinched his already well-abused nipples as she slowly rode him up and down, rocking her hips forward and back. Soon, her pace quickened and she huffed and grunted as she bounced her hips up and down, crashing on his steel-hard cock.

Jim was groaning, doing whatever he could not to cum. He never trained his body for this; he never thought he would be in such a situation, and it took every ounce of energy he had in him to stave off the release he so desperately wanted. Julie, knowing he had little left holding him back finally took pity on him.

"Jim, cum for me! Cum! Cum now!" she demanded as she pinched his nipples hard. With a guttural cry of ecstasy, Jim blew his load into the condom, and the mere thought of having such power over such a strong-willed, reserved man, sent Julie over the edge as well; not to mention the long, thick cock she engulfed with her hot pussy felt nothing short of euphoric for the sex-starved ENFP. Both came with ferocity and passion until they could bear no more. His mistress collapsed on his nude body, both were breathing heavily and her tongue gently licked his ear as she rested on him.

Julie, still sweating and exhausted, undid the bindings on his limbs and then wrapped her arms around her lover. "That...was..." Jim couldn't find the words, but she knew, and she felt the same.

Her answer was to kiss him once again passionately and seemingly without end. When their lips finally unlocked, she kissed his forehead gently. "So, are you still looking to kick me out?" she asked.

"Yes," he said seriously, but he couldn't conceal his smile for long.

"I guess I'll have to give you even more reasons to keep me tomorrow," she said.

"I'm looking forward to your sales pitch," he said.

"I'll make you an offer you can't refuse," she said, nibbling his ear as they snuggled in each other's arms and drifted into blissful, exhausted sleep.

Story 3: Maid to Serve

The hunger drove her to do it. She pondered the idea for some months now, but whether it was her pride or simply fear, she always convinced herself there would have to be another option. Begging for scraps of food from the noblemen and shopkeepers in the village was no way to get by, and twenty-one-year-old Faye Dunham knew this was her best option to put food in her belly and a roof over her head. She could have opted for a life on the dark streets, spreading her legs for coin, but the beggar had a modicum pride left in her. The thought of whoring her body to sleezy drunks and horny sailors sickened Faye to her very core. With jobs scarce, indentured servitude was the best option for the young beauty.

She knew how to cook reasonably well, her skill at cleaning earned her some coin in the past, and she had a way with hemming dresses and stitching quilts. She thought of becoming a seamstress, but the fire which killed all those girls in the textile factory last month sent shivers down her spine. She would rather face the whip of a cruel master or mistress for ten years rather than burn to death for a few bent pennies.

The process of becoming an indentured servant was frighteningly simple. She merely showed up, gave her signature, and was given a routine exam to check for lice, tuberculosis and other ailments or defects which would make her a less than savory addition to any proper home. She stood on a platform with dozens of other men and women looking to pay their debts or earn a meager living. Most looked miserable, victims of their poor choices, but Faye had a feeling of hope and optimism that things would finally get better, not worse. A defiant and hopeful smile crept on her face.

That sense of optimism began to fade when portly men with bushy mustaches began examining the candidates. A rotund man with a top hat stared Faye lustfully. He licked his lips and snapped his suspenders against his chest. "Oy, she's a ripe young one, ain't she?" he asked the lead seller.

"Name's Faye Dunham. Twenty-one. Lived on the streets but came back clean and healthy. Beggar. Says she can cook a variety of dishes and that she cleans, shines shoes and hems," the lead seller, a bland, tall man with slicked-back gray hair said an unenthusiastic tone. To him, Faye was just another commodity to be sold; nothing more.

"I hope she cleans more than dirty dishes and laundry, if you get what I mean," the bulbous man laughed heartily.

"They're yours to do as you please for ten years. Fuck them, beat them, put them up to grinding work; I don't care, as long as I see my coin," said the bored merchant of misery. He checked his pocket watch and sighed.

"How much for the runt?" he asked.

"Five hundred," the seller replied.

"She's a bit short; not very useful for a servant to fetch me things. Four hundred."

"Four seventy-five. She's a solid candidate. She's healthy, has nice tits, and minds her manners."

"I'll give you six hundred," a woman's voice entered the fray. Faye looked up and saw a stunningly beautiful, elegant woman primly dressed in black. Her hair was as black as her dress, pinned in a bun and under a black bonnet. Her face was pale but all the warmth resided in her hazel eyes. She looked at Faye with little emotion, other than fierce determination to obtain this girl.

"W-well, I'll give you seven hundred!" the fat man countered.

"Eight," she said coolly.

"Nine!" he roared.

"A thousand," the lady in black said.

"A thousand...for that little mouse? Keep her!" the fat man said, then turned his eyes on a blonde woman down the row and said "hello gorgeous, and how much are you?"

"One thousand for Faye Dunham, and she's yours for ten years," the lead seller said.

"Very well," the woman replied icily. She produced twenty gold coins worth fifty shillings each, signed the documents and kept the ownership papers.

"Move along lass, go with your new owner," the lead seller ordered Faye.

"Follow me," the woman in black said. She led Faye to an all-black horse drawn carriage and told the driver to take them home.

Faye sat opposite her new mistress and kept her eyes downcast.

"My name is Lady Adriana Marcello. I have purchased your services for the next ten years. You will be fed, you will be clothed, you will have a warm bed and earn two shillings per day. You will be paid the accumulated total of your schillings at the end of each month. You are to address me as Lady, Mistress, or Madame. Your role will be to serve me my meals, repair my dresses and clean my chateau. This means dusting, mopping, wiping, laundry, linens, windows, and assisting Mr. Lemons with attending to the horse. You will assist the cook staff in preparing breakfast, lunch, tea, supper and cocktails. You may also be required to be at my service for other tasks...as they arise. Do I make myself clear, Faye?"

"Yes, Mistress," she said dutifully.

"Good. You seem like an eager, hard-working young woman...but know that there are consequences for failing to follow orders, disobedience, dereliction and desertion. Those consequences include physical punishments. Do I make myself clear again?"

"Perfectly, Lady," Faye replied, daring not to look at the gorgeous woman. She couldn't have been much older than Faye's twenty-one years, but even if she had been younger than her, the elegance, command, and dignity she carried would have instantly granted her earned respect from the subservient woman.

"I'm not a cruel Mistress, Faye. I want you to feel welcome in my chateau, but I do expect obedience. Those who obey get rewarded; isn't that right, Mr. Lemons?"

"Yes, Mistress," the carriage driver said right away.

"Good boy," she cooed, pleased with his compliance.

"Thank you, Mistress!" he replied.

The ride from the hustling, bustling city with its coal stained sky slowly gave way to the pleasant meadows and rolling hills of the countryside. Forests crested some of the taller hills and dotted some of the flatlands. Butterflies were busy collecting nectar from the myriad of colorful flowers scattered over the serene landscape. Everything seemed colorful, except Mistress Adriana. Her dark ensemble and quiet demeanor set a dark tone for an otherwise cheery ride.

The arrived at her chateau. The slate-colored boulders making the outer walls of the abode seemed to match the dour dress and mood of the mistress. Ivy grew on the ancient walls stretching from the ground to the highly angular, patinaed copper roof. Iron wires ran in a medieval lattice-pattern over the windows, giving the imposing structure the look of an inescapable prison. Though it wasn't a grand estate, it was certainly larger than a single woman, a servant, two cooks and a driver really needed. Several bedrooms, a library, study, office, and grand ballroom completed the elegant if drab home.

"I'll show you to your room," Mistress Adriana said. She walked ahead of Faye who struggled to keep up with her mistress's quick, prim steps. Adriana unlocked a door and showed a modest room to Faye. It held a bed, a nightstand, a dresser and a chest. The dresser had a mirror and a wash bowl, a hairbrush, a pitcher and a pewter cup. The nightstand had a few sheets of paper, a quill pen and ink well, and a candelabra.

"This is amazing, Mistress!" Faye said with genuine joy. It was a far cry from sleeping on whatever rags and paper scraps she could scrounge up in the alleyways on cold winter mornings. Even if the servant's quarters were spartan and somehow even drabber than the rest of the dwelling, the room was *hers* and Faye felt important and dignified to have her own private room. Faye's only possessions were the tattered clothes on her back, so she felt like she had stepped up in society to have her very own room with a bed and all these accessories.

"Your clothing is nothing short of disastrous. The drawer should have a maid's outfit or two. I assume you can tailor it to your size and fit?" Mistress Adriana asked.

"Yes, Mistress, most definitely," Faye eagerly replied.

"Good. Also, you are filthy. I expect you to take a bath at once. This is the way to the bathroom. There is running water, but you must heat it in the hearth lest you wish to take a frigid bath."

"I understand, Mistress," Faye said with a curtsey.

"When you are finished, return to your room, but do not get dressed. The slavers and sellers aren't nearly as thorough as I'd like them to be when they examine their goods."

"Oh…y-yes, Mistress," Faye said. Her face blushed with the command, but she was bound to follow any and all requests from her Mistress. Failure to comply would result in justifiable punishment.

Faye was awed by the bathtub's running water. She brought a few of the buckets to the hearth and warmed them in the fire, adding the scalding water to the cold water until a pleasant balance was achieved. And there was soap! Genuine, real soap which smelled of lavender and rosemary. She soaped her body down. Her pert, ample tits with their dark nipples and areolas were covered in the lather. Faye found herself very self-conscious of her body now. Every stroke of the bar of soap seemed exciting. She just figured it had to do with the fact she would be presenting herself to the young, attractive Lady.

Soon, she finished and dried herself with a towel provided by her mistress. She found her way back to her room where Lady Adriana waited impatiently for her arrival. "You took an awful long time to finish. Seeing as this is your first day, and you were rather filthy, I will let it go...*this time*," she said. "Now, drop the towel."

Faye let the towel fall to her feet. She stood with her hands behind her back, presenting her body to any and all inspections her mistress had in store for her. Adriana opened Faye's mouth and tilted her head toward the window to catch the light. She examined her teeth and gums, running her finger over them and her tongue. Faye couldn't understand why she felt wetness between her legs; she was certain she dried off there.

Adriana grabbed both of Faye's breasts and jiggled them in her hands. The sensation sent waves of strange pleasure through the peasant girl's body. She didn't understand why she was feeling the way she did, but she didn't want it to stop. Adriana tweaked the young woman's nipples, twisting them roughly. Faye softly whined but said nothing in protest. Her mistress crooked an eyebrow with surprise at the maid's pain tolerance.

Crouching down, now, the tall woman forced Faye's legs apart. She examined her sex. It was hairy, matching the brown hair on Faye's head, and to Adriana's shock and delight, little beads of moisture, which weren't from the bathtub, had collected on the hairs. She kept the grin to herself, but she realized the thousand schillings she paid for the woman may have actually been a bargain. Turning Faye around, she spread her butt cheeks apart and was satisfied the girl had cleaned herself off well enough.

Standing back up, Adriana looked down at her property and said "very well. Go on and try on the outfit."

"Yes, Lady Adriana," Faye replied dutifully. Adriana sat on the bed as her servant changed into the outfit. Aside from it being slightly loose at the collar, the outfit was remarkably well-tailored to her already.

"Very good. Now, it's getting close to tea. Go down to the kitchen and set the table.

Then, I want you to see if you can be of any use to the cook staff. When the food is ready, you will serve me my meal. The cook staff will advise you what to do."

"Yes, Mistress," she said.

"Good girl," Adriana said. Faye couldn't understand why, but the two simple words sent those same strange tingles to her groin again. She hoped she wasn't still leaking, dampening her new outfit. It had been far too long since she had felt those feelings from her body with the constant threat of starvation taking precedent, but she now felt those strange, pleasurable sensations twice in one day.

Faye helped the two cooks in the kitchen, but Mistress Adriana watched from afar. Her eyes were always on the newly acquired maid. Faye couldn't quite tell if her mistress was watching her like a hawk to correct her for any errors she made or if it was because she was drawn to the supple, young servant. Faye concluded it may have been a bit of both. It was unusual for womenfolk to pursue other women in these parts, but not unheard of. Faye herself was convinced she preferred the feminine form over the male body, but few women would even consider indulging in such acts with her, so she kept her desires a secret known only to herself, and she rarely ever indulged in those thoughts.

Mistress Adriana seated herself at the head of the grand table. She looked both imposing at the large, empty table, yet also painfully lonely. Faye diligently served the meal, course by course, waiting with her hands behind her back, standing just a bit to the side of the table.

"More wine," Adriana demanded. Without a word, Faye quickly filled her glass from the carafe. The beautiful, elegant lady ate her dinner in silence, save for the few commands she barked out to the servant. Finally, the meal was over, and Faye was allowed into the kitchen to feed herself. The cooks explained to her what was available and off-limits to the servants in terms of food, so she settled for some bread, hard cheese, and cured meats along with some inexpensive wine.

When she finished eating, she nearly jumped out of her skin, for Adriana had been standing behind her in the kitchen entrance the entire time, watching her in silence. "Come, girl. There's something I must do to you."

"Yes, Mistress," Faye said. The servant had no idea what her mistress meant by those words, but she dared not talk back to the powerful woman who towered over her by at least half a foot. She followed the lady back to her elegant bedroom where Adriana dug around in her dresser and produced an intimidating object.

"You are my property. As such, you must be easily identified as bound to me. This leather collar will remain around your neck until your tenure as an indentured servant is up. Only when you bathe or are around water shall I remove them, to avoid rust around the buckles and rings or the leather wearing out."

"Y-yes, Mistress," Faye stammered nervously. She knew what she was getting into when she signed the papers trading her freedom for the security of food, clothing, shelter and some money, but the shackles and collar made it all seem more real now.

"Kneel before me," Adriana ordered Faye. She dropped to her knees before her mistress. "Look up at me." Faye's doe-like blue eyes looked up at her Mistress's hazel eyes. "I'm going to tell you this once, Faye. You lucked out. There are many masters and mistresses far worse than I am to their indentured servants. I am fair. That does not mean I will not punish you. I can and *will* punish you if you are disobedient, negligent, lazy, or disrespectful. My punishments can be exquisitely unique and memorable. But I do not go looking for excuses to punish my servants. Do not confuse fairness with weakness, for if you break the rules, I will break your skin, and perhaps worse. Am I clear?"

"Yes, Mistress," Faye said humbly.

"Keep looking into my eyes as I collar you," Adriana said. The black, leather collar had rings on it to attach chains or rope, and Adriana's symbol of a raven clutching a heart in its talon's was the only silver item at the center of the collar. "Kiss it," Adriana demanded, placing the collar against her lips. Faye reluctantly kissed the bird symbol. A small half-grin briefly appeared and vanished on Adriana's lips. She affixed the collar around Faye's delicate neck and latched it shut, then inserted a lock around the loops, securing it to her for as long as her mistress deemed necessary.

"Very nice," she said to herself, softly. She then spoke louder. "My neck and shoulders ache from today's ride. You will rub them thoroughly."

"Of course, Mistress," Faye said.

The collared servant followed her Mistress to a lounge chair in the bedroom. Adriana sat in the chair and removed her clothing, save for her undergarments. Faye gawked at her beautiful, pale skin for a moment, but quickly positioned herself to rub her mistress's back and shoulders.

"Don't stop rubbing my back, neck, and shoulders until I tell you," Adriana instructed, and leaned forward for Faye's hands to have access to her creamy, white skin. For the third time in a day, Faye's crotch began to moisten, and the strange but pleasurable feelings in her gut and loin grew once again.

Feeling the warmth and smoothness of Mistress Adriana's skin against the palms of her hands was more pleasurable for Faye than she would have ever imagined. It was a pleasure to massage her mistress and an honor for her to see her exposed as she was. Faye's fingers found knots and sore spots in her mistress's back and neck. Her delicate fingers slowly and methodically worked out the problem areas, and she heard Adriana let out a few soft moans of approval.

Faye tried everything in her power to resist the strange, pleasurable feelings she felt as she continued to gently rub the skin, muscles and sinews of her owner. Even thinking of the ugly men who swindled unsuspecting townsfolk of their money, or the rats scurrying in the alleyway, did little to temper the desires she felt for her mistress. Her mind was almost lost, drifting into thoughts of pleasuring this gorgeous governess.

"That's enough, Faye," she heard Adriana say, and the servant looked disappointed to be stopping. "You may go to your room and get some rest. You've had an exhausting day today, but tomorrow will not be any easier, nor will any of the days ahead of you for the next decade. Get some rest and be ready to serve my every whim."

"Yes, Mistress," Faye said humbly.

"The next ten years will not be easy for you, but you will accumulate wealth over that time, you will learn new skills, and you will be well provided for. I paid a handsome sum for your services...do not make me regret my purchase."

"I will be certain to please you in any and every way possible, Mistress," Faye said, to which Adriana raised a curious eyebrow once again.

"We shall see about that, shan't we?" Adriana countered icily.

"I promise to do as you command, Mistress," Faye said.

"Promises are dangerous, little one. Be careful when you make them. Good night."

"Good night, Mistress," Faye said, retiring to her meager but comparatively comfortable quarters. Faye felt luxurious sleeping in her new bed. She no longer needed to sleep among the rats and strays or beg for discarded crusts of bread. Whatever cruelty her mistress could dream up would be worth it, in Faye's eyes.

The next morning, Faye woke up eager and excited to start the day. Sleeping in a warm, comfortable bed for the first time in many years was invigorating in and of itself, but being able to serve the beautiful and graceful Mistress Adriana made it all the sweeter to wake up with purpose and clarity. Everything felt...*right*.

The young and perky maid began her duties by helping the kitchen staff prepare breakfast for Mistress Adriana. Eggs were boiling, toast was being warmed in the hearth, and the kettle whistled its readiness to join tea leaves in the pot. Faye had already set the silverware and china for her mistress when Adriana descended the impressive stairs of her manor.

The noblewoman wore a flowing, dark green dress which hid her leg movements in such a way that she seemed to float down the stairs like a graceful spirit. Faye couldn't help but stare at the elegant lady as she made her way to the table. She snapped out of it long enough to pour the mistress her tea.

"How do you take it, Mistress?"

"Sweet...and creamy," Adriana said as she looked Faye directly in the eye. Faye's hands began to tremble. A tiny bit splashed out of the cup, onto the saucer and splattered on Adriana's hands. "You've made me wet," Adriana said. Though the tea was hot, her mistress didn't so much as flinch.

"I'm so sorry, Mistress," Faye said, immediately reaching for a towel, but Adriana grabbed her wrist.

"There are worse things in life than making a woman wet, Faye," Adriana said.

"Please, let me clean it from you," Faye begged.

"You'll have enough to do today. Worry not, little one," her mistress said dismissively.

Faye carefully fetched the rest of Adriana's breakfast for the wealthy woman. As the elegant mistress ate a piece of toast, she saw Faye waiting off to the side to attend to her mistress's needs.

"Come, sit," she instructed her maid, pointing at an empty chair to her right.

"B-by you, Mistress?" Faye asked with trepidation.

"Yes, of course. Do you see anyone else at the table?" Adriana replied with a smirk.

Faye took her seat and looked down at the silverware set for a guest which did not exist. She dared not make eye contact with Adriana, but her mistress would have none of it.

"You know, it's an absolute shame..." she began.

"What is, Mistress?" Faye asked when Adriana didn't continue.

"You have such beautiful eyes, but you hide them from me every chance you get by staring down at the floor, or in this case, the table."

Faye turned her head up slowly and looked at Adriana with her mournful, soulful, deep blue eyes. Adriana's heart skipped a beat. Even though she was very dominant and well-composed, it was like staring at a work of Davinci or finding the lost city of El Dorado when she looked into Faye's ocean-colored irises.

She cleared her throat, regaining her composure and said "that's better. Now, tell me about yourself, Faye. What was your life like before you decided to give yourself to indentured servitude?"

"M-my life?" she stuttered, earning a single nod from her mistress. Faye went on. "I was born into a house of seven others. Five brothers, my mother and my father. My father was a shoemaker, my mother raised us and sold matches on the streets. When she died of cholera, my father was never the same. He beat my brothers daily, though he spared me the rod most days. He found opium and the devil was in that smoke. When he tried to...*tried...to*...with me, but my eldest brother, Thomas, stepped in and clocked my father straight in the jaw just as my father dropped his pants. He told me to run...and I ran. I've never been back home since," Faye said. Her hands trembled and her eyes filled with tears.

"You poor thing," Adriana said, and uncharacteristically poured a cup of tea for Faye, the mistress serving the servant.

"I learned to survive on the streets. My brother Thomas always told the rest of us to work hard, and I did. I scrounged up things people threw away and I fixed them to sell to whoever had the coin. I worked odds and ends jobs, cooking, cleaning, repairing linens, but I never sold my body! Not once!" she said proudly.

"So, you never laid with a man?" Adriana asked.

"No, never, Mistress," Faye said earnestly.

"Do you regret not doing so?"

"No, not at all, Mistress! I...personally don't find them to be..." she let her voice trail off, fearing she said too much.

"To be..." but Adriana pressed her.

"Very kind, Mistress," Faye said, happy she thought of something on her feet which didn't betray her desires to her owner.

"Do you feel you would find more...kindness...in the company of a woman?" Adriana asked, and the small droplets of tea on Adriana's hands didn't compare to how Faye spilled her entire cup on the table.

"I'll clean it, I'll clean it!" Faye said in a panicky voice.

"That can be done later. Follow me, little one," Adriana ordered Faye sternly. The indentured servant followed closely behind her mistress, terrified of what might happen next. Adriana led them to her bedroom. She looked at her maid's out fit and pressed her hand by Faye's thighs.

"You're wet. You should slip out of that outfit."

"Yes, Mistress," Faye whispered a terrified reply.

"I've already seen your body, love. You have no reason to fear being nude around me. I own every inch of you, anyway," she said matter-of-factly.

"Y-yes, Mistress," Faye said, and it was then she truly realized the extent of her decision. Her Mistress could do anything she wanted to her. The thought was terrifying yet strangely exhilarating to the servant. Faye removed her clothing and stood nude in front of the elegantly dressed lady. She shivered; not from the cool air on her naked skin, but from excitement and nervousness. Her mind was racing with reasons why she shouldn't be feeling stimulated, but her body was craving everything which was happening, and it was beyond anything she could have imagined.

"Sh-should I change into another outfit, Mistress?" Faye asked.

"Silence," Adriana ordered. It wasn't barked out or cold in tone. It was a simple command she expected her servant to follow. Faye immediately fell silent in front of her mistress.

Faye shivered again as Adriana walked around her nude body like a lioness casually sizing up its hopeless prey. She ran her fingers over Faye's nude back, tracing her long nails over her pale, soft skin. Faye's breath quickened, her nipples were erect, and her pussy was absolutely drenched.

Lift your arms high above your head. Good girl, just like that. Adriana breathed in Faye's scent from the back of her neck. She kept her face close to the space between her neck and shoulders.

When Adriana whispered in Faye's ears, it was as if bolts of electricity coursed through the servant's body. "I have a feeling...you'd much prefer a woman touching your body than a man."

Adriana's hands reached around and cupped Faye's soft, supple breasts. She held them in her hands, feeling their weight and the silky smoothness of the warm skin around her tits. Her thumbs began to rub the submissive maid's already hardened nipples. A soft mew of pleasure escaped Faye's lips. Adriana's lips caressed Faye's neck and the servant felt her mistress kiss her neck gently. The Lady gently squeezed Faye's breasts, tugging on her nipples from behind. She began a rhythmic tugging motion, as if milking the udders of a cow, but with more finesse and gentleness.

Faye's knees felt weak and she only prayed they didn't give out while her Mistress fondled her so lovingly. Adriana's tongue began exploring the shorter woman's neck and shoulders, leaving evaporating saliva in her wake and causing goosebumps on already chilled skin. Adriana's right hand wandered down Faye's ribcage, down her belly, down to the indentured servant's slopping wet pussy.

"Oh! You must have spilled some tea down here, too! You're all wet," Adriana said, then took her fingers to her mouth and licked off the juices. "Wait a second, that's not tea. Faye...why didn't you tell me you were so sweet? I wouldn't have needed any sugar earlier!" Faye didn't respond; she was petrified, too mortified to speak.

Faye felt Adriana's left hand take a similar route down her body, but instead of visiting her drenched pussy, it caressed her round, supple ass. Her right hand found its way to her right butt cheek and both hands began to alternate between caressing, kneading, groping, and swatting her perfectly shaped ass. Faye protest-whined when those same hands began to spread her cheeks wide.

"Mistress, please, no," she begged.

"I'm sorry, what did you say?"

"Please, not my bum, it's so sensitive!"

"Thank you for your honesty in informing me that, little one. I always appreciate when I get freely divulged information like that. Without any hesitation, Adriana spread the cheeks even wider, revealing the little, tight fleshy star of her anus. Faye trembled, and Adriana could feel her whole body shake as she held her butt cheeks spread wide. The servant girl's pussy positively dripped all down her thighs. "Stay exactly in that position, little one." Adriana ordered Faye.

She went to a drawer and fetched several devices custom made by the local blacksmith. A bar with shackles on each end was the first thing the mistress used on her servant, and she attached them to her dainty ankles. Faye's legs were now spread and unable to close with the spreader bar attached.

"Mistress, what are you doing?" Faye asked timidly.

"You shall not question me, nor my actions. Is that clear?"

"Yes, Mistress," Faye said in a squeaky voice. She wondered if she had made a terrible mistake giving away her freedom for the next decade. It was barely her first full day in servitude and she was already bound and naked by her mistress's hand. Even though her mind raced with doubt, her body betrayed her and craved every minute of the humiliation and bondage.

Mistress Adriana then attached shackles to Faye's wrists, securing the other ends with a chain which led to hooks in the ceiling that the servant hadn't noticed adorned numerous points throughout the elegant room. On closer look, she saw metal loops attached to many spots on the floor and walls, as well, and she shivered once again in fear. What kind of dark desires did this mistress of hers have, anyway?

"Stay right there, don't go anywhere," Adriana said with an evil smirk as she left the nude, bound maid alone in her room. Faye stood naked, shackled and spread for several minutes alone in her mistress's bedroom when Adriana finally returned. She couldn't see what it was Adriana brought in the room, but whatever it was, the submissive maid knew it would likely be scary.

"When it comes to horses," Adriana said in an academic voice, "the notion is, there are two ways to motivate the beast. The carrot or the stick. One can either reward the equine with a carrot for exhibiting the desired behavior, or one can correct the horse through the use of the whip to discourage a bad behavior.   The best horse trainers say both are needed to produce the best results. Luckily for you, I happen to have both," Adriana said showing Faye a riding crop in one hand, and an actual, raw carrot in the other. For some reason, the riding crop didn't scare her half as much as the carrot did.

"Please, Mistress, I beg of you…"

"The first measure of business will be to correct these issues of insubordination; speaking when not spoken to, for instance," Adriana said, and with the conclusion of her sentence, she let a sharp crack of her crop find Faye's delicate buttocks. The young, submissive woman yelped with pain and shock.

Faye's world had turned upside down. She awoke in her own bed with food in her belly and fresh clothes on her skin. Now, she was bound and naked, receiving swats from her mistress's riding crop, feeling the warm throb of her ass with each blow. Adriana grinned at how easy it was to mark Faye's fair skin. Each impact left the distinct, reddish-pink imprint of the broad leather end of the crop. It was as much about the fear as it was the pain. Some smacks didn't even land on her ass; rather, she whacked the leather against the bedpost, creating the same cracking noise. Faye jumped as violently with the fake hits as with the real ones.

Tears streamed down Faye's cheeks, but it wasn't just her eyes which leaked. Her pussy dripped like a flower vase which sprung a leak. Her inner thighs glistened while her nipples stood erect. Faye's ass was extremely sensitive, and she couldn't understand why the stinging swats were turning her on more forcefully than anything in her life prior. When the merciless thrashing was complete, Faye's entire rear was red as a cherry.

Adriana unhooked the restraints holding her wrists up and the much taller, more muscular dominatrix dragged Faye to her bed, attaching the wrist restraints to hooks which could fully rotate in the headboard, allowing the slave girl to be rotated on her back or belly as often as needed. Her tanned ass made laying on her back all the more uncomfortable, and Faye writhed and wiggled, trying to find a position which didn't sting as much. But, much to Faye's relief, Adriana undid the spreader bar to her ankles, allowing her legs to move freely again.

"Hmm, the hair around your nether region just will not do," Adriana clucked disapprovingly, leaving the bound woman secured to her bed as she once again departed the bedroom. The mistress returned with a bowl of hot water, a brush, shaving powder, and a glimmering straight-razor.

"No, please Mistress!" Faye whispered faintly.

"Hush. Now Faye, I'm going to require you to lay perfectly motionless. We don't want to nick that precious little quim of yours," she said, mixing the shaving powder and some warm water in a little dish with the brush until a frothy salve was formed. Mistress Adriana brushed it on the pubic hairs of her servant and she twitched and jumped at the sensation. "You'll have to be a lot stiller if you don't want to be bleeding at the end of this," warned Adriana.

"Yes, Mistress," Faye squeaked. Her throat was dry and her fingers trembled. Her eyes focused on the tools her mistress used. She felt the cold steel scrape away years of hair from her groin. Her mistress had deft hands and was surprisingly gentle given the beating she had just inflicted upon Faye. Faye's lips trembled with nervousness and her nostrils flared but she managed to keep her body still as she watched her mistress turn her sex smooth.

"Mm, there we are," she said, wiping the area with a cloth dipped in the warm water. "For the next ten years, you will be kept smooth. Now, it's time for a little taste."

"A taste?" Faye asked meekly, but Adriana decided to answer with action rather than words. The governess crouched between Faye's forcibly spread legs and positioned her face over her cleanly shaven groin. Adriana's long, slender fingers spread Faye's soft, glistening, pink, fleshy labia lips open, inviting Adriana to dart her tongue inside the lithe woman's extremely tight sex. Faye sucked in air through her teeth and whimpered; not out of pain, but out of stifling the desire she had for all this to happen.

Faye couldn't believe how much more sensitive she had become since being denuded of her hair. Adriana's tongue generously explored her entire nether region; there wasn't a place she was not willing to taste. Faye let out several contented sighs as Adriana's tongue grew teasingly ever nearer to her clit. She didn't want the servant girl to cum...just yet.

Adriana was having a hard time concentrating. The taste of her servant girl was intoxicating. Her scent was clean, like rainfall over a meadow. Her taste was an exhilarating balance between subtle sweetness and saltiness, but mostly, just clean and watery. The governess found it remarkable how a woman living on the streets was so pure and fresh tasting, but it only added to her alure. She was wet; of that there was no denying. Faye seemed like an endless fountain of juices cascading from her tight quim, and her mistress was positively drenched in the face.

"Well now, my little servant, you've had a taste of the stick. I do believe it's time for the carrot," Adriana said crooking an eyebrow knowingly.

"No, please Mistress, beat me, but please, anything but that!" begged Faye.

A leathermaker crafted it for her. It was not something one could merely buy at the shop. There was craftsmanship involved in the strange piece of equipment, and when Adriana laid it on the bed next to the bound, submissive maid, Faye could only speculate its purpose.

Adriana began to undress from her complicated wardrobe. Her flowing, green dress was carefully set upon the armoire, and she approached Faye wearing stockings and a bra, and panties which seemed to reveal far too much for a woman of her stature. Faye was mesmerized by Adriana's beauty. Her pale, creamy skin, her taut and shapely legs, her large but pert breasts, in stark contrast to her raven hair. She slipped one leg through the leather device she had custom-built for her, then the other. A series of buckles and latches kept the harness secured at her pelvis. A leather ring in the middle where her groin was, was what Adriana used to secure the small carrot. She pulled the strap on the buckle of the leather ring, securing the carrot in place. Mistress

Adriana now looked as if she donned a small, orange penis due to the carrot strap-on.

"No, please!" begged Faye.

"I think you should take it in your mouth, get it nice and moist so I can enter your tight little quim easily enough," Adriana said, kneeling in front of Faye. She put the peeled carrot to Faye's lips. "Suck on it."

Reluctantly, Faye accepted the sweet vegetable in her mouth. Adriana began rocking her hips back and forth, thrusting the vegetable-toy in her maid's mouth. Faye whimpered and gagged, making slurping noises as she tried to accommodate this violation of her mouth. Adriana increased the tempo and ferocity, and Faye couldn't handle it anymore. She bit down on the carrot and devoured the vegetal cock.

"That...was a foolish thing to do, little one," Adriana said. She sprung from the bed to her drawer of toys and fetched a small, rubber penis. "This was crafted with rubber from Siam. Do you know where Siam is? Of course, you don't. All you need to know is, this special cock was handcrafted for me. It's not too wide or too large; perfect for your tight entrance. Now, I spent a great deal of time and money having this crafted for me, I won't risk have you bite off the rubber. No...instead...I'm going to mount you as is. You seem wet enough, anyway!"

"Please, Mistress," Faye begged hoarsely. In her mind, she didn't want; her lips made the words that she didn't want it, but her body betrayed her once again, and she felt a burning need to be humped by this beautiful woman of gracefulness and power.

Faye's ass was still red from the beating Adriana gave it. The mistress looked for the reddest, sorest part to grab on to as she positioned herself behind the woman's shaven genitals. Adriana's "cock" now hovered an inch below Faye's labia, and it already glistened from the drops of secretions leaking from her vagina. "The first time is always a bit unpleasant. You will learn to love it...in time. Well, you'll have ten years to get used to it, at least." Adriana waned the servant.

Faye felt the head of the rubber cock press against her sopping wet pussy. She sucked air in as Adriana slowly entered her. Even the diminutive size of the rubber cock felt full and enormous in her abnormally tight twat. She felt tears stream down her cheeks the further Adriana pressed on. The rubber strap-on was now as deep as it could go. Adriana's own groin pressed against Faye's and the feeling of the heat emanating from her mistress was unlike anything she could have imagined sex with another woman would be like.

Adriana parked the rubber rod in her submissive maid's pussy and just let it rest against her tight tunnel walls. She fondled Faye's beaten and abused, perfectly-shaped ass. Digging her finger nails into her skin and leaving little red marks on top of the already reddened skin only added to the art of her creation. With the cock still wedged up Faye's tight vagina, Adriana licked her index finger a spit gently on Faye's star. She slowly inserted her finger up the servant's equally tight asshole, and Faye yelped with surprise, then immediately apologized for the outburst. Adriana ignored both. She fingered the woman's ass gently all while the rubber cock nestled snuggly in Faye's Vagina. Eventually, she pulled her finger out, along with the rubber cock.

Faye sobbed softly as Adriana began pulling out. She hoped that was it for the punishment, but a quick thrust back in made it clear it was not. Adriana now began thrusting back and forth as the rubber cock invaded Faye. Faye yelped once again and couldn't even come to her senses to apologize this time. Adriana still didn't care. She was lost in pounding the supple woman's gorgeous pink nether region.

The maid could hear each smack of Adriana's groin slapping against her gushing pussy. The sounds were absolutely lewd, noises her ears had never heard before. The unrelenting thrusts started to hurt less and became more pleasurable with each new entry. Her loins felt like they were on fire. A strange, vibrating, tingling feeling spread from her groin to her stomach and traveled down her legs. The sensations were bizarre, but Faye didn't want them to stop. In fact, her mouth sided with the rest of her body and betrayed her.

"Oh, yes, Mistress!" she squeaked.

Adriana chuckled with confident satisfaction. She knew Faye would learn to crave the artificial cock, that she would do anything to be fucked like a piece of meat at every opportunity. She could see it in her eyes. Though Faye acted shy and reserved, the mistress knew what lurked beneath those innocent expressions.

There was a woman, in Faye, whose desires had until then, gone unmet. Adriana knew she was unlocking secrets unbeknownst even to her servant girl. These desires were there all along, and she was forcing them out with four inches of hand-crafted rubber attached to a leather harness. It didn't even matter if Faye would be a mediocre maid; her real duty was to lie spread for her mistress to use and abuse at her whim. The spilled tea was a trivial mistake, now. Faye was soaking the mattress much like she soaked Adriana's dress.

"Mm, oh yes, don't stop," cooed Faye, and Adriana slap-grabbed her ass and thrust as hard and as fast as she could. Fay was twitching; her body shivered and her secured hands made fists. She took pain remarkably well, thought Adriana as she madly pounded her servant into a powerful, earth-shattering, gushingly wet orgasm. "Yes, yes, yes!" cried Faye; she squeaked with each impact and grunted when she finally came.

"I'm not quite finished with you yet," Adriana warned, turning her over once again with the rotating hooks securing her bindings. Faye was still breathless from the pounding she had received, but it was certainly not the time to rest. On her back now, Faye looked up at her mistress who smiled wickedly.

"I know how you taste, but I think it would only be fair to return the favor. First, clean off the mess you made on my precious toy," Adriana ordered, shoving the rubber dildo against Faye's lips. The servant girl tasted her own juices on the rubber cock and understood why Adriana enjoyed her taste so much. She sucked on the cock until her mistress had enough. "Good, good. You take all of my abuse so splendidly, little one."

"Thank you, Mistress," Faye said, catching her breath.

"I know you've never pleasured a woman before, so I'll be lenient on your performance. That being said, I want your tongue to work on me in much the same way I gave mine upon your quim. Is that understood?"

"Yes, Mistress," Faye said timidly yet obediently. Adriana slipped out of the strap-on and presented her sex to Faye's mouth. Though she shaved Faye down there, a true mistress need not give the same courtesy to their submissive, so she left her bush intact. The dominant woman took her fingers and spread her folds to display her sex in front of captive Faye's face.

Her odor was feminine and decisively so; it was stronger and slightly muskier than Faye's. Faye drank in her mistress's scent deeply. The heat from her pussy radiated to Faye's face and for a brief moment, she was hesitant, but a stern look from the domineering woman quickly brushed away any fears the twenty-one-year-old woman had of tasting another lady's most private of areas. Slowly, hesitantly, Faye stuck out her tongue and began tasting her mistress.

Though she was nowhere near as wet as Faye, Adriana's pussy was delectable and better than anything the servant girl could have hoped for; it was a pleasure to pleasure her. Whereas Faye squirmed with pleasure at her mistress's tongue, Adriana forcefully began grinding her crotch into Faye's exploring tongue and lips. The bound woman's face was glistening from the juices Adriana rubbed off on her. Though she didn't moan, Adriana sighed contentedly at the remarkably good job her servant-slave was doing on her pussy.

"Get used to that taste, little one; you'll be expected to pleasure me like this any time I desire it. Your body is mine to do as I please, yours is to obey my commands and do your utmost to please your mistress. Your happiness will be tied to mine. I reward good behavior with many types of treats, but I punish bad behaviors with little room for mercy," Adriana stated even as she was getting eaten out. Her voice was controlling, soothing, and sultry.

Faye was starting to explore Adriana's nether region with reckless abandon. Her tongue wildly and enthusiastically prodded, poked, and pleasured her mistress with such randomness, it was hard for Adriana to keep up. For her first time, the servant was remarkably adept in Adriana's eyes. Desperate to maintain composure and control in the presence of her slave girl, Adriana grabbed on to Faye's hair and held her by the hair as she frantically grinded and gyrated against Faye's all too eager tongue.

"Oh my," Adriana moaned, and she felt embarrassed for uttering even a single word, let alone two, in front of Faye. The sounds of Faye's tongue eagerly slurping up Adriana's drippings was positively lewd, but neither had any reason to fear interference from the rest of the staff. The cooks and other attendants were all busy with their tasks, and one newly acquired maid was sweating more than any of her servants.

The two, simple words of affirmation sent Faye into a frenzy; she wiggled her tongue frantically and in patterns neither would have never dreamed of. Secondary to her own pleasure, even the strange tingles she got from receiving pain and the mind-shattering orgasm she received from the pounding, Faye realized pleasing her mistress was the most erotic thing possible. Seeing Adriana's looks of bliss and ecstasy was far more important than receiving pleasure for herself, and it now became her single mission to make her mistress cum like Faye did.

Adriana bit her full, dark-red lip, closed her eyes and ran her fingers through her servant's hair. Adriana had slept with a few women in her time; she even managed to dominate them and put them through humiliating scenarios like she had with Faye, but only Faye seemed to relish every moment of it, and this was intoxicating to the governess. Every stroke of the whip, every thrust with the rubber cock, and every wiggle of her delicate tongue on even more delicate, nerve-filled folds of moist flesh, Faye showed no signs of being disgusted by any of it.

Even in her blissful state, Adriana thought to herself with an internal chuckle that punishing a girl like hers may prove difficult if every punishment turned into pleasure for the maid. She didn't have much time to dwell on the thought, though, because a warmth emanating from her groin spread to her belly and thighs as little ripples of pleasure seemed to course through her veins like a drug. Adriana's breath quickened, her heart raced, her toes splayed and her grip on Faye's hair was almost cruel. Adriana jerked her head from side to side as the most powerful orgasm of her life shook her to her very core.

Several moments passed where the two did nothing but breathe together. Their sweat-drenched bodies and oozing vaginas made their bodies glisten. Both women had hair which was scattered and messy, and neither seemed capable of forming a single word for minutes as they caught their breaths. The Lady recovered first.

Adriana took a key from a string around her neck and undid the shackles attached to Faye's wrists. She slid down over Faye's naked body and embraced her indentured servant. "You did a very good job, little one," Adriana said, kissing her forehead. She then locked her lips with Faye's and the two kissed passionately for several minutes, tasting the faint flavors of each other's lust in their mouths. Adriana's hands gently caressed Faye's bare body. There was a marked difference between how she tenderly loved her slave girl from just a matter of moments prior when she tanned her ass and thrust her rubber cock deep into the tight vagina of her lover.

"Thank you, Mistress. Pleasing you was the best part," Faye eagerly said.

"I'm glad to hear that, because it will become one of your duties over the next ten years."

"It will be my honor and pleasure to make you happy, Mistress," Faye said, earning a soft kiss from Adriana as they embraced each other and drifted to blissful sleep. Faye was only happy to give her freedom, her mind and body to this wonderful Mistress. She would live to serve, love to serve, and was made to serve.

www.ingramcontent.com/pod-product-compliance
Lightning Source LLC
Chambersburg PA
CBHW031320130726
47988CB00007B/2918